Magic Molly

The Invisible Bunny

HOLLY WEBB

ILLUSTRATED BY ERICA JANE WATERS

Scholastic Children's Books
An imprint of Scholastic Ltd
Euston House, 24 Eversholt Street, London, NW1 1DB, UK
Registered office: Westfield Road, Southam, Warwickshire, CV47 0RA
SCHOLASTIC and associated logos are trademarks and/or
registered trademarks of Scholastic Inc.

First published in the UK as *Molly's Magic: The Invisible Bunny* by Scholastic Ltd, 2009
This edition published by Scholastic Ltd, 2017

Text copyright © Holly Webb, 2009
Illustrations copyright © Erica Jane Waters, 2009

The rights of Holly Webb and Erica Jane Waters to be identified
as the author and illustrator of this work have been asserted by them.

ISBN 978 1407 17132 6

A CIP catalogue record for this book
is available from the British Library.
All rights reserved.

Printed by CPI Group (UK) Ltd, Croydon, CR0 4YY
Papers used by Scholastic Children's Books are made
from wood grown in sustainable forests.

1 3 5 7 9 10 8 6 4 2

This is a work of fiction. Names, characters, places, incidents
and dialogues are products of the author's imagination or are used
fictitiously. Any resemblance to actual people, living or dead,
events or locales is entirely coincidental.

www.scholastic.co.uk

www.holly-webb.com

For Alice, with love

Chapter One

The Birthday Party

Molly pulled on her favourite pink
jeans, and her T-shirt with the puppies
on it. She'd bought it with her pocket
money the last time Mum had taken her
shopping. The puppies looked so like her
friends Star and Stella, the wish puppies,
that she hadn't been able to resist it.

Molly smiled at the puppies. She hadn't
seen Star and Stella for a while, and she
hoped they weren't wearing out their
new owner too much. Mrs Hunter was

quite old. Molly had helped to bring Star and Stella back together after Mrs Hunter had bought Star, without knowing that she was a magical wish puppy and needed her twin. Molly had been the only person who could tell what was really wrong with Star when she had come into Molly's dad's surgery. Sometimes being able to talk to magical animals was a big help!

Molly grinned at herself in the mirror.

By the time Kitty's birthday party was finished, she was bound to be covered in cake and ice cream, but at least she could start off looking nice!

Kitty was downstairs already, in her new purple birthday dress, with no less than six *I am 4!* badges on. Mum had tried to persuade her not to wear them all, but Kitty was being stubborn, and it *was* her birthday, so she'd got away with it.

"Is he here yet? Is he here yet? When *will* he be here?" Kitty was jumping up and down by the living room window, which looked out on to the lane. "Can you see him, Molly?"

Molly looked out. "No. Who?"

"The Amazing Albert! The magician!" Kitty stared at her as though she were mad. Then she went back to the window.

"Oh! Look at that car! That has to be his car!"

A beautiful old red Rolls Royce was purring slowly up the lane, and turning into the yard outside Larkfield Vets, Molly and Kitty's home. Kitty raced back to the kitchen door and out into the yard, watching as the Rolls parked outside their dad's surgery. An elderly man got out, wearing a red tailcoat, with the most enormous white moustache Molly had ever seen. He spotted Molly and Kitty at once, and bowed, very low. Kitty was delighted, and curtseyed back, holding out her purple dress.

Molly's dad came out to help the magician carry in all his boxes, and Kitty's guests started to arrive too. Molly was kept busy showing them where to put their presents, and telling everyone where

to go, but she couldn't help peeking out
into the back garden every so often. She
hadn't been very excited when Mum said
there would be a magician, but that was
before she saw the Amazing Albert. He
just looked – well, magical.

It was a wonderful afternoon, really

en though it was the beginning
ber. The magic show was set
the garden, with all the children
sitting round on shiny red cushions that
the magician had brought with him. Dad
had joked that he must have a magic car,
he'd fitted so much stuff into it, but the
Amazing Albert had just smiled.

The magician was now wearing a tall,
scarlet top hat as well. He looked brilliant,
and all Kitty's friends gasped when he
made bunches of flowers appear out of
nowhere (he gave them to Molly's mum).
Then he juggled with flaming torches,
and rode on a unicycle. At last, he blew
the torches out, and crouched down
closer to the children.

"Do you like my hat?" he asked, in a
very serious voice, and everyone nodded.

He swept it off his head, and held it

out in front of him. "Would you like to see what's inside it?"

"A bunny rabbit!" Kitty gasped excitedly, and the magician laughed.

"Not yet. Look, completely empty. But now..." He put in his hand, and felt around, frowning. "Where's she got to?" Then he poked his nose into the hat, and everyone giggled. "Snowdrop! Where are you? Aha!" And he pulled out a beautiful snow-white rabbit, her fur sparkling in the sunshine. "This is Snowdrop!"

The rabbit stared round at the children, her nose twitching with interest. She was the prettiest rabbit Molly had ever seen, with big dark eyes, and almost silvery-looking fur.

"Now, Kitty, as it's your birthday, Snowdrop and I would like you to help us with this next bit. And perhaps your big sister too," the Amazing Albert added, looking thoughtfully at Molly. "That's it, come on out here. Now, I shall put Snowdrop back..." He laid a red silk handkerchief over the top of the hat, and then whisked it away. "And you can see, everyone, the hat is now empty! Now, Kitty and Molly, see if you can lift her out again."

As soon as Molly reached into the hat with Kitty, and touched Snowdrop's silky fur, she knew that she wasn't just any rabbit. There was a wonderful warm, tingling feeling rushing through her fingers, and the hat seemed to be full of pink sparkles – her fingers were glittering.

And when they pulled Snowdrop out of the hat, she wasn't a white rabbit any more.

She was pink!

Molly gasped, and everyone in the audience *oooh*ed with delight. Snowdrop looked up at Molly, and Molly was *almost* certain she winked. Then she went back to staring innocently out at the audience.

Molly could hardly sit still for the rest of the magic show, she was so excited. Snowdrop simply had to be magical.

Not everyone was as convinced as Molly was, though. Her cousin Louis was sitting at the back next to her, and he just looked bored. He was a couple of years older than Molly, but they got on pretty well.

"Isn't she brilliant?" Molly whispered excitedly.

Louis looked at her disgustedly. "Oh, come on, Molly. You don't believe it's real magic, do you? It's all a trick. It's obvious!

You can't really make a rabbit change colour!"

Molly just stared straight ahead, smiling a little. Maybe not. But a *magic* rabbit could do it all by herself...

At the end of the show, Albert invited everyone to come and stroke Snowdrop. Molly was desperate to go up, but she hung back, hoping that all the others would want to go and start tea, and she might get a moment to talk to Snowdrop without anyone listening.

They were the only ones left in the garden now. Shyly, Molly went up to the Amazing Albert's table, where Snowdrop was sitting while the magician packed away his tricks. Was it her imagination, or was Snowdrop staring at her too?

"Please may I stroke her?" Molly

asked politely, and the magician smiled.
"Of course!" He twirled his moustache,
watching Molly thoughtfully.

Molly put out her hand to stroke
Snowdrop's ears, but the white rabbit
shook her head, and jumped straight into
Molly's arms instead. Molly gasped – she
could really feel Snowdrop's magic now.
A wonderful warmth was running all
the way down to her toes, like she was

drinking sparkly hot chocolate.

"You *are* magic!" Molly whispered
happily. "I thought so!"

"Well, you are too!" the rabbit
promptly replied. "Didn't I tell you?" she
demanded, looking over Molly's shoulder
at the magician.

"Yes, yes, I know, she can hear you
talking." He was nodding delightedly.
"Snowdrop said she thought you were
different, when you pulled her out of the
hat. And of course, when she came out
pink, I knew there was something special
about you. Snowdrop doesn't turn pink
for many people."

"Can you do other colours too?" Molly
asked Snowdrop, impressed.

Snowdrop looked smug. "Of course.
Any colour you like!" she boasted. "Even
stripes!"

"Only on a good day," Albert reminded her. "At that party last week you were a very plain brown, *and* you smelled of fish."

Snowdrop sniffed, and twitched her ears as though she didn't like to be reminded. "He was a very unpleasant little boy," she said loftily. "He was picking his nose. Molly is *nice*. Look!" Snowdrop wrinkled her nose, and closed her eyes, and then her tail turned purple.

"Oh, that's fantastic!" Molly giggled.

"So Molly, tell me, have you always been able to talk to animals? Snowdrop's never spoken to anyone but me before, this is a most exciting day for us!" Albert twirled his moustache with one finger, making it curlier than ever. He looked really delighted to have met Molly.

Molly beamed at him. "No, I only

realized a few weeks ago. I met a magic kitten called Sparkle, and then two wish puppies, Star and Stella. But that's all. I've never met a magic rabbit. And I only know one other person who can talk to animals – Sparkle's owner. She's a witch who lives in Larkfield Wood."

Albert nodded. "It's a rare gift, and very special. Oh my goodness!" He checked his watch. "Snowdrop, we must go! We have another party, Molly. I'm sorry we can't stay, but I'm sure we'll see you again."

Molly helped him carry his boxes to the car and waved them off, then she wandered slowly back to the party, smiling happily to herself.

She'd met a witch's kitten, and two wish puppies, and now a magic rabbit. A rabbit who could change colour, and vanish into a hat. Albert was right – it was a wonderful day!

Chapter Two

The Hiccupping Bunny

Molly wasn't sure how she was going
to see Snowdrop and Albert again. She
wished they hadn't had to dash off so
quickly. Albert had said they would meet
again, but Molly couldn't see how. It
was all a bit disappointing – she'd met a
gorgeous magic bunny, and she'd hardly
had a chance to talk to her! She couldn't
stop thinking about rabbits all week,
and her teacher told her off for drawing
rabbits on her science worksheet.

On Friday afternoon, Molly ran over to the surgery to see if her dad wanted any help. She looked interestedly round the waiting room, and wondered why the man in the brown jacket looked so familiar. He was bending over a box on his lap, but when he looked up, Molly recognized the moustache at once – it was Albert!

"Molly!" He sounded very pleased to see her.

Snowdrop popped her head out of the box at once, her whiskers twitching with delight. "Hello!" she whispered, as Molly crouched down next to her.

"Snowdrop?" Molly's dad was looking round the surgery door. "Oh! Aren't you...?"

"The Amazing Albert, yes." Albert smiled.

"Kitty's still talking about you!" Dad waved them in. "So, what's wrong with Snowdrop? She seemed very healthy at the party. Beautiful condition."

Albert lifted Snowdrop out and cuddled her. "It sounds silly, but – she keeps getting the hiccups. It started a few days ago, soon after Kitty's party, actually. They go on for so long, and I'm just a bit worried about her. She's never had them before."

Molly's dad looked intrigued. "Well, I've never had that one before." He looked at Snowdrop thoughtfully. "No other symptoms, just hiccups? I might have to go and look that up... Would you mind waiting a minute?"

As soon as Molly's dad had gone, Albert gave Molly a worried look. "I couldn't really tell your father, Molly, but it's *not* just hiccups..." He stroked Snowdrop anxiously. "She disappears! Not always, but every so often, she hiccups, and then she vanishes! I don't know what to do!"

Molly looked at Snowdrop, expecting her to be worried too, but Snowdrop almost looked as though she was smiling. "It's fun," she whispered to Molly.

"Yesterday we did another birthday party, and Snowdrop started hiccupping inside my top hat. I could feel it shaking! And then when she was supposed to disappear, she did, but she didn't come back!" Albert shook his head worriedly. "I had to pretend it was part of the show."

Snowdrop wriggled crossly in his arms. "I did come back, in that special present," she reminded him. "Everyone was very impressed!"

"Yes, but it was in the pass-the-parcel," Albert explained to Molly. "And they were impressed, but that little girl's mother was very confused, Snowdrop. She couldn't work out where the box of crayons had gone. Nor can I, for that matter."

Molly could just imagine what her

mum would have said if she'd found a rabbit in Kitty's pass-the-parcel. "And you really don't have any idea why?" she wondered, watching as Snowdrop wriggled out of Albert's arms, and went to explore the rest of the surgery.

"No," Albert sighed. Then he murmured, very quietly, so Snowdrop couldn't hear, "And I can't help worrying, what if next time she doesn't come back?"

Just then Molly's dad came back in, still holding a very large book on rabbits and everything that could possibly go wrong with them.

"I *think* she may just have an upset stomach," he said. "Not too serious. I'll give her some soothing medicine, and you need to keep a careful eye on her diet. No lettuce!"

Albert looked relieved, but then he frowned. "Is there any chance it could be catching?" he asked worriedly.

"Well, it could be a virus, yes. Like stomach flu in humans," Dad agreed.

Albert shook his head. "Oh well. I suppose I'll have to cancel," he said sadly.

"What's wrong?" Molly asked. "Do you have another party?"

"No," Albert sighed. "A big magicians' conference, in Edinburgh. I'd been quite looking forward to it, but it starts tomorrow and I won't be back until

Tuesday. I can't risk Snowdrop giving hiccups to all those other rabbits, it just wouldn't be fair."

Snowdrop was scrabbling at his trouser leg, and he picked her up and stroked her ears sadly. She gazed round at them all, her eyes anxious.

"Snowdrop could stay here at the vet's!" Molly suggested excitedly. "We'd look after her for you, then you'd still be able to go."

"Oh, Molly, hang on," Dad said, shaking his head. "Normally I'd say yes, of course we could, but we're really busy this weekend, and Jenny's on holiday, remember? Jenny's our veterinary nurse, Albert. I'm really sorry, I'm just not sure we can fit in looking after Snowdrop too."

"I'll look after her!" Molly said eagerly.

She was standing on tiptoe, gazing hopefully up at her dad and Albert.

"I could, honestly. I know loads about rabbits, I really do."

"I'm not sure, Molly..." Dad murmured doubtfully.

"I could! Dad, I'm nearly eight, you know! Lots of my friends have pets. I'm not too young, I promise."

"It *is* only for a few days," Albert put

in, looking at Molly's dad pleadingly. "I'm sure Molly would look after Snowdrop beautifully. They seemed to get on very well at the party."

"And if Snowdrop's tummy upset got worse, Dad, she'd be in the right place!" Molly pointed out.

Snowdrop wrinkled her nose, and gazed at Molly's dad too.

Molly was almost sure she heard a faint tinkling sound, like little bells, and the air seemed to shimmer pink for a second. She caught her breath. Was Snowdrop doing magic?

Dad shook his head slightly, as though he was feeling dizzy. Then he looked thoughtfully at Molly. "Oh, all right..." he sighed. "But you're going to have to be very responsible, Molly."

Then Snowdrop winked at her. There

was no doubt about it this time. Snowdrop
had magicked her dad into saying yes!

"Wonderful!" Albert cried, hugging
Snowdrop. "I'll bring Snowdrop's hutch
round tomorrow morning before I leave."

"We could put it in the shed, couldn't
we, Dad?" Molly suggested. She really
wanted her dad to see how much

she knew about looking after animals. "Rabbits shouldn't be outside all night now it's getting chillier. And we get foxes around here. She'd be much safer in the shed. I can go and tidy it up, Dad! You'll get a tidy shed too!"

"Mmm." Dad still didn't sound convinced, but at least he wasn't saying no.

"Thanks, Dad," Molly said, putting an arm round him. "Honestly, I'll look after Snowdrop so well. You'll see!" Molly just couldn't keep the smile off her face. She went to stroke Snowdrop's nose, and whispered, "You're coming to stay with me!" It was so exciting!

Snowdrop gave her whiskers a delicate little shiver, and they glittered pink for a second. She looked excited too.

Molly sighed happily. At last she was going to have the chance to show Mum

and Dad how well she could look after
a pet. It was almost as if her special wish
puppy wish for a pet of her own was
starting to come true!

Chapter Three

Snowdrop Settles In

Molly got up super-early on Saturday
morning to tidy the shed ready for
Snowdrop's hutch. It wasn't much of a
fun job. The shed was full of gardening
tools, and seed packets, and spiders. Kitty
kept trying to help, and then shrieking
and running away whenever she saw
even a leg of a spider. But it was worth
it to have a pet, even if Snowdrop was
borrowed, and only Molly's for three days.

Snowdrop's hutch was huge. It almost

filled the back seat of Albert's car, and Dad had to help him carry it in. They set it up in the shed, and then Albert took Snowdrop out to say goodbye.

"Be good!" he told her firmly. "Don't be naughty for Molly. And *please* try not to hiccup!" he added in a whisper. Then he handed her to Molly, and looked worriedly at them both. "I do hope you'll be all right," he murmured. "I've never left her with anyone else before."

"You'll be late if you don't set off soon," Snowdrop told him. "Molly and I will be fine. Won't we?" There were pink sparkles fizzing round her ears, and she had a look of mischief in her eyes.

Molly nodded happily. "We really will!" she promised. She hadn't noticed Snowdrop's mischievous glance.

Albert handed her an enormous bag

of carrots. "Her favourite..." he muttered.
Then he rushed off to his car, without
looking back.

Snowdrop was Molly's now!

It was wonderful, having a pet, especially
one who could talk back! Molly spent
most of the day in the garden with
Snowdrop, chatting, although of course

they had to be careful when Mum or Dad or Kitty were around. Snowdrop was very funny. Molly soon discovered that she liked to have things her own way, and she was quite fussy. She liked eating daisies, but only the yellow middles, and she insisted that Molly had to pick the petals off one by one, as they tasted better that way. Molly tried pulling all the petals off at once when she wasn't looking, but Snowdrop spat that one out, and gave her a reproachful look.

"Sorry..." Molly said, trying not to laugh. Snowdrop's face was so funny. After that, she didn't try to argue when Snowdrop demanded that her stomach medicine had to be fed to her drop by drop on wafer-thin slices of peeled carrot. It was easier just to do as she was told.

"Molly! Teatime!"

Molly jumped up. "Oh, that's Mum. I'll

pop you back in your hutch, but don't
worry, I'll come back out to see you after
tea."

Snowdrop nodded, and hopped back
into her sleeping quarters. Molly was sure
that the hutch was actually bigger on the
inside, as it seemed to have at least four
rooms. "I shall have a rest," Snowdrop said
grandly. "This has been rather a tiring
day." She lay down on her back in the

hay, with her paws in the air, and closed
her eyes. "You could bring me some
grated carrot later, perhaps," she suggested.
"As a little bedtime something. . ."

After tea, Dad came back out with Molly
to check that Snowdrop was settling
down well in her new home. Molly
grinned to herself when Dad said this.
Sometimes she wished she could tell him
that some of the animals spoke to her.
But she didn't think he would believe
her – he would say she'd imagined it.
Right now it would be fun to be able to
say that Snowdrop was fine – but she'd
asked for grated carrot for supper, and
she didn't approve of the view from her
hutch, because the lawnmower was too
grubby. Molly had promised to wipe it.

"I wonder if that medicine's working

yet?" Dad said thoughtfully to Molly as they walked down the garden. "Have you noticed Snowdrop hiccupping at all today?"

"No." Molly shook her head. "Maybe she's better. It would be great to be able to tell Albert we'd cured her, wouldn't it?" Molly skipped ahead excitedly as Dad stopped to see how his flowerbeds were looking. She would love to be able to welcome Albert back on Tuesday with the news that Snowdrop was all better.

But just as she opened the shed door – it was sticking a bit, so it took a minute – Molly heard a hiccup. Not very loud, but definitely a *hic!* She sighed. Oh dear... There was another one, and another, and then a flash of golden light lit up the hutch. Molly caught one glimpse of Snowdrop's startled face, peeping out of the wire front of the hutch, and then there was a loud *pop!* and she disappeared.

Then Dad walked into the shed – to find Snowdrop gone.

Molly was peering into the back of the hutch, trying to work out if Snowdrop was still there, just invisible, or if she'd actually *gone* somewhere.

"Molly, what are you doing?" Dad

asked, sounding surprised. "Snowdrop's not going to like you sticking your head in her hutch like that! Can you get her out for me, so I can check her over?"

Molly closed her eyes tightly, then opened them again and looked back in the hutch, hoping that Snowdrop would have miraculously reappeared. But she hadn't.

"No."

Dad blinked. "What?"

"I can't get her out ... she, umm ... she isn't here, Dad..." Molly twisted her fingers worriedly. What else could she say?

"But – but where is she? Molly! You can't have lost her, we've only had her for a day? What happened?" Dad sounded really cross. "Did you leave the hutch open?"

"No! Of course not!" Molly said, her

voice hurt. She was far too sensible to do that!

"Molly, you must have done, how else could she have got out? I knew this was a bad idea." Dad shook his head. "Right, you search in here, see if she's hiding behind any of the gardening things, and I'll go and look outside. I just hope she hasn't got out of the garden, we might never find her." Dad rushed out on to the lawn, and Molly followed him, trying to explain, but what could she say? Dad wasn't going to believe that Snowdrop had vanished all by herself.

Molly walked back into the shed, and stared anxiously into Snowdrop's hutch. "Snowdrop! Snowdrop!" she whispered. "Please come back! I'm really worried about you, and Dad's so cross, he thinks I let you out. Please come back as soon as you can!"

Nothing happened. Molly could hear Dad calling crossly in the garden and running up and down, searching under the bushes.

"Please, Snowdrop!" she whispered again.

All at once there was another flash of golden light, and Snowdrop was back. She was sitting on top of her hutch now, looking slightly dazed. "*Hic!*" she said loudly. And then, "Hello, Molly!"

"Sssshhh! My dad's here, he's looking for you. He thinks you're lost. Please will you get back in your hutch, he's so cross!"

Snowdrop sighed, and let Molly slip her back into the hutch, just as Dad came striding back into the shed. "There's no sign, Molly. This is why Mum and I were worried about you having a pet. You have to be so careful – hey, where did she come from?"

"She was there all the time, Dad!"
Molly said, trying to smile, and shutting
the hutch door *very* tightly. "I think she
was hidden behind her hay bed, I just
couldn't see her!" She felt a bit guilty,
because it wasn't strictly true. But after
all, she hadn't left the door open, and
Snowdrop hadn't *really* gone out of the
shed, had she?

"But I looked too..." Dad muttered.

"She just wasn't there. You are one tricksy bunny," he told Snowdrop sternly. "I'm getting a bad feeling about this weekend." He sighed. "Don't be long, Molly, all right? And make sure you close that hutch up tightly! I don't trust that rabbit, at all..."

Chapter Four

Snowdrop at School

Molly tried to get Snowdrop to explain where she'd been, so she'd be able to find her if it happened again, but Snowdrop said she didn't know.

"It was somewhere sparkly," she said, not very helpfully. "And it smelled nice."

It wasn't a lot to go on.

Molly just had to hope that Snowdrop wouldn't get hiccups when Dad was around. She didn't think he'd believe the story about losing Snowdrop in the hay *again*.

"I wish I knew how to cure you,"
she told Snowdrop on Sunday afternoon.
They were sitting in the shed doorway,
Snowdrop on Molly's lap, her eyes
blissfully closed as Molly stroked her ears
over and over.

"Mmm."

Molly got the feeling Snowdrop wasn't
really listening.

"Mum tells me to hold my breath and

count to ten when I get hiccups, have you tried that?"

"Rabbits aren't good at holding their breath," Snowdrop said, stretching her front paws out lazily, so that she was flopped all across Molly's lap.

"When I got hiccups at Grandad's house once, he gave me a spoonful of sugar to stop them, but I don't think sugar's good for rabbits..." Molly sighed.

Snowdrop's ears twitched with interest. "Perhaps we should try..." she said hopefully.

Molly giggled. "Snowdrop, you are so greedy!"

"I only want to cure my hiccups," Snowdrop protested, trying to look innocent.

Molly tickled her ears. "I'll miss you when I'm at school tomorrow," she said sadly.

Snowdrop sat up at once. "School? You mean you won't be here?"

"Well, no, tomorrow's Monday! I have to go to school, Snowdrop, even though you're here. I'm really sorry. You don't get days off because of rabbits."

"Well, you should..." Snowdrop muttered grumpily. "I don't like being on my own, it's very boring. I wanted to go to the conference, and I wasn't allowed, and now you're leaving me too!"

Snowdrop sulked on and off for the rest of the day, until Molly brought her a whole bowl of grated carrot before she went to bed. Then she let Molly kiss her nose, and even said sorry for being so bad-tempered.

But the next morning Snowdrop had had an idea. "Can't I come to school too?" she asked hopefully.

"No!" Molly said, sounding horrified. "We aren't allowed pets at school, ever! I mean, we do have a school guinea pig, but we can't bring our own pets into school. I'm sorry, Snowdrop. I just came to fill up your food and water bowls. And I brought you some beautiful carrots, see..."

Snowdrop sniffed. But then her eyes brightened, and she picked up one of the carrots in her teeth. As Molly took out the bowls to refill them, Snowdrop hopped up on top of the hutch, where Molly had left her lunch box. Snowdrop wasn't just any rabbit after all. She had learned lots of useful tricks with Albert, and she was quite capable of opening a lunch box, without even using magic. She quickly dropped the carrot inside, and glanced back down at Molly, who

was still making sure there were lots of
sunflower seeds in her food bowl.

"Albert said you really liked them, so
I'm giving you some extra ones, OK?"

Snowdrop blew a waft of glittery,
golden breath on the carrot that made it
go all sparkly. She twitched her nose in

a satisfied sort of way, and nudged the
lunch box shut. Done. "That's hardly any!"
Snowdrop protested, peering down at her

food bowl. "Lots more than that!"

Molly shook a few more in. "There you go! You've got loads now. Have a nice day, and I'll be back by afternoon snack time! See you later!"

"Goodbye, Molly!" Snowdrop watched her carefully shutting the hutch door. She was planning to see Molly a little sooner than Molly thought...

Rabbits seemed to keep popping up at school that morning. The maths problems were about how long it would take how many rabbits to eat a field of lettuces, and two of Molly's friends had new rabbit pencil cases. It made Molly jittery. She really hoped Snowdrop was behaving herself!

At lunch time, Molly sat and stared at her lunch box. She didn't really feel hungry. But she could feel one of the

teachers watching her, so she opened it
up at last.

There was a carrot inside.

A whole carrot, with the green feathery
leaves still on the top. Molly blinked at
it. Mum sometimes gave her carrot sticks
in a little pot, but not a whole one! It
looked awfully like one of the carrots
she'd given Snowdrop that morning...

As she stared, the carrot started to

sparkle – just little golden glimmers round
the leaves. Molly gulped, and grabbed
it, hiding it in her lap. Luckily all her

friends were complaining about the test Miss Fraser had given them that morning (which Molly couldn't even remember) and hadn't noticed. Molly quickly took off her cardigan, and put it over the carrot. She had a horrible feeling she knew what was about to happen.

She was right. There was a funny little noise, rather like a hiccup, and a flash of golden light, which luckily was mostly hidden under Molly's cardigan. Then the cardigan wriggled, and Snowdrop's silvery-white nose peeped out.

"Hello Molly!" she squeaked excitedly. "I've come to school too!"

"How did you get here?" Molly whispered, tucking Snowdrop's ears back under her cardigan. "We mustn't let anyone see you!"

"I put a finding spell on the carrot,

so I could follow it when I hiccupped.
It was very clever of me. Aren't you
impressed?" Snowdrop sounded smug.

"Of course I am, but we're going to get
into trouble. I told you, we aren't allowed
pets!" Molly looked round anxiously, but
no one seemed to have spotted that she
was talking to her cardigan.

Snowdrop wasn't listening. "I'm soooo
hungry! It was hard work, that spell," she
moaned.

"Eat the carrot!" Molly said crossly.

"I'm bored with carrots now. I'd like something else. Maybe some lettuce. Have you got any?" Snowdrop started to creep out from under the cardigan, and Molly grabbed her in horror.

"No!"

"OW!" Snowdrop squeaked loudly, and everyone looked at Molly. Molly looked behind her, trying to pretend she didn't know what the noise was either. Then there was another *pop!* and a flash, and Snowdrop wasn't huddled under Molly's cardigan any more.

So where was she?

Knowing Snowdrop, Molly thought, she would be looking for food. She'd wanted lettuce. Molly looked round to see if anyone had lettuce in their sandwiches. She had to get Snowdrop back before

someone spotted her... Then she noticed
a spot of white over by the dinner
queue – Snowdrop had found the salad
bar! She was sitting happily on the edge
of a big metal tray of lettuce, nibbling
away blissfully.

Molly stood up, wondering how on
earth she was going to get Snowdrop

out of there without anyone seeing her. But she was too late. There was a sudden scream, and one of the dinner ladies threw a ladle at Snowdrop. "It's a rat!" she yelled, then she fainted with horror, collapsing in a heap behind the counter.

Snowdrop jumped into the air in panic, then there was an enormous *pop!* and she disappeared completely, leaving everyone wondering just what was going on.

Molly ran across the room, hunting for Snowdrop, but she couldn't see her anywhere. It didn't help that half the girls in the school (and some of the boys) thought Snowdrop had been a rat too, and were standing on their chairs screaming.

Molly spent the whole of lunch time searching, but Snowdrop was nowhere to be seen. She'd got such a fright,

Molly just didn't know where she might
have gone. She was really hoping that
Snowdrop had jumped back to her hutch,
where she would feel safe. But when
Molly finally got back from school, and
raced down the garden to the shed,
there was no welcoming squeak from
Snowdrop's hutch. It was quite empty.

Molly sat down on the step, blinking
away tears. Crying wouldn't
help. Snowdrop
was gone – and
Molly had no
idea how to get
her back.

Chapter Five

The Sparkly Spell

Molly sat staring out into the garden, desperately trying to think of places Snowdrop might be. She couldn't give up! She just hoped that Snowdrop wasn't frightened, or hurt.

There was a rustling in the bushes, and Molly looked up sharply. It was only a blackbird, but Molly got up to search round the garden anyway. Snowdrop didn't seem to have an awful lot of control when she disappeared without expecting to. Maybe she'd aimed for her hutch and missed?

She was just peering under the wheelbarrow that Dad had left out, when Kitty came up behind her, very quietly. "What are you doing?" she asked, and Molly jumped and banged her head on the wheelbarrow.

"Nothing!" she snapped crossly. But it was lucky that it had been Kitty who caught her, not Mum or Dad. She mustn't let them find out that Snowdrop had disappeared! She had to find her first!

But as Molly realized this, Dad came walking down the garden. "Mum wants you, Kitty. Hi Molly, how was school? Have you been to see Snowdrop? Did she miss you today?"

"Mmm!" Molly didn't know quite what to say. She cast an anxious glance down to the shed, at the bottom of the garden.

"I'll just have a quick look at her before tea." Dad carried on down the path.

"Oh, no, she's all right!" Molly gasped out.

"It's OK, Molly, I'm sure she's fine — you've done so well looking after her." Dad put an arm round Molly's shoulders. "I have to say, Molly, I'm really impressed.

You've been very responsible."

Molly felt sick – she'd been hoping that Dad would say something like this, and she'd been waiting for her parents to notice how well she was looking after Snowdrop, but why did it have to be *now*? When Dad was just about to find out that Snowdrop was gone. Molly suddenly knew that she couldn't – mustn't – let Dad see the empty hutch.

But what was she going to do? Suddenly the magical locket that Sparkle the kitten had given her seemed to grow warm around her neck under her school shirt. Molly put her hand up to it. It felt glittery and buzzy and special, and Molly took a deep breath. It was like a magical message from Sparkle, telling her she had to do a spell – but Molly had never done magic on her own before.

Dad had let go of her and was strolling on, muttering to himself about needing to cut the grass, it was full of daisies. He was right.

The daisies made Molly think of Snowdrop, and her fussy daisy-eating. Her eyes pricked with tears. Molly knelt down and picked a handful of daisies, hurriedly pulling off the petals one by one.

Dad was almost at the shed now.

Molly closed her eyes and threw the handful of daisy petals up in the air, whispering, *Stop him!* to herself. They seemed to hang in the late afternoon light for a few seconds, fluttering and shimmering silver. Then they floated down, and some of them landed in Molly's dad's hair. He stopped, and ran one hand across his face, looking confused.

"Oh, Molly, now what was I meant to be doing? It's always the same, you get down to the end of the garden and forget what you went for." He sighed, and wandered slowly back to the house.

Molly stared after him, with her mouth hanging open. That was the first time she had done magic all by herself – and it had worked! A thrill of delight ran through her – she felt so proud!

But there was no time to celebrate, she still had a missing bunny to find...

Worn out from searching all afternoon, Molly cried herself to sleep that night. She couldn't help imagining Snowdrop, lost and alone somewhere, probably frightened, with no idea how to get home. Albert was coming home tomorrow, and he would be really looking forward to seeing her. How could Molly tell him Snowdrop was lost?

But in the middle of the night, Molly woke up with a jump. She'd been dreaming of carrots. Feathery-leaved, orange and green and silver-sparkly carrots. Just like the one that Snowdrop had used in her naughty spell to appear at school. Molly sat up in bed, staring into the darkness, her breathing fast and

trembly with excitement. The carrot — she
still had the carrot! It was in her school
bag, wasn't it?

Molly slid out of bed, tiptoed across
her floor, and made for the stairs as
fast as she could. She crept down them
in the darkness, feeling her way by
hugging the banister. There was a little
moonlight shining through the glass
in the front door, so she could almost
see. Her school bag was sitting in the
hallway, and Molly ferreted through it.
There was something round, and cold —
no, that was a water bottle. . . But here
it was! She could feel the cool, feathery
leaves, and the tingle of magic as her
fingers closed round it. Molly dashed
back up the stairs, and curled up back
in her bed, holding the carrot in shivery
hands.

"Snowdrop! Snowdrop!" she whispered. "Where are you? Find your way back!"

There was a flash of golden, glittering light, like there had been at school, and Molly caught her breath excitedly, sure that Snowdrop would come bouncing on to her bed.

But she didn't. No bunny hiccupped, and the carrot was just a carrot again.

Chapter Six

A Cure For Hiccups

Molly woke to hear Mum calling her
from the doorway.

"Molly! Molly! Wake up! You haven't
overslept, have you? You must have had a
busy day at school yesterday. Get dressed
and come down quickly, Molly, Albert's
here! He drove all night to get back and
see Snowdrop, he was missing her so much."

Molly blinked sleepily. Albert. Snowdrop.
It took a few seconds for the names to
mean anything, then it all flooded back.

Albert was here to fetch Snowdrop, and Molly didn't have her!

The spell hadn't worked, and Molly had fallen asleep again eventually, still clutching the carrot. She felt awful. She could hear Albert's voice downstairs, talking to Mum and Dad. He sounded happy and excited, as though he'd had a great time at the conference. There was an eager tone to his voice as well. Obviously he was waiting for Molly to come down and take him to see Snowdrop. It was nice of him to wait.

Molly sniffed, burying her nose in her pillow. She didn't want to get up and tell everyone the truth. Oh, why hadn't it worked? The carrot was on the pillow next to her, the long green leaves tickling her chin.

And giggling. Molly opened her eyes, slowly. She was fairly sure that even

carrots with spells on them didn't giggle.
But magical rabbits did, and their whiskers
were tickly and tingly...

"Oh, do wake up!" a soft little voice
muttered in her ear. "Come on, Molly,
haven't you missed me?"

It *had* worked! Molly sat straight
upright, almost knocking Snowdrop off
her pillow. "Where *were* you?" she gasped.

Snowdrop shuddered. "I don't know! It was horrible, it was *very* far away, and it was all dark. I didn't like it at all. I was so happy when I heard you calling me. It took a while to get back, that was all. I'd been trying to look for Albert, but it was hard when I'd never been to that Edinburgh place."

"Ohhh!" Molly breathed, hugging Snowdrop delightedly. "I thought it hadn't worked! I was so worried about you!"

Snowdrop nudged Molly's chin with her nose, in a sorry sort of way. "I shouldn't have followed you to school, Molly, it was my own fault I got lost in that dark place, and you saved me. Albert will be very grateful."

Molly jumped out of bed. "Did you hear? Mum said he's downstairs. I need to get dressed and get down there."

"And you need to get me back into my hutch!" Snowdrop pointed out. "Albert wouldn't mind me being up here, but I don't think your mum would like it. Can I take the carrot? I'm starving!"

Molly was pulling on her school uniform. "Can't you magic yourself back?" she asked, halfway inside her shirt.

Snowdrop was silent for a minute. Then, "I don't think so," she said doubtfully. "I think something's happened... I'm sure I can disappear with you or Albert to help me, but I don't think I can do it on my own any more. The hiccup feeling's gone, and that's what was making me jumpy..."

"You're not hiccupping any more? Really?" Molly picked Snowdrop up and stared at her thoughtfully. "But that's amazing! You're cured! I wonder how, though?"

Snowdrop gave a little shiver. "Well, I don't *know*, but I think that horrible woman throwing something at me had something to do with it. Every time I want to hiccup, I can't help thinking of her! Uugggh!"

Molly laughed. "Of course, a fright! That's the best cure for hiccups there is! It's what Dad always tries to do when me or Kitty have them, only he's useless at it and he just makes us laugh. I can't believe we solved the problem without even trying!"

Snowdrop nodded. "It's a pity, I shall miss those funny magic jumps. But Albert will be relieved. Please, Molly, I do want to see him so much. If you hold me, and we both think of my hutch, I'm sure I can get there. Then you can go down and fetch him for me."

"OK." Molly held Snowdrop tightly, and thought of the pretty, blue-painted hutch, the sweet-smelling hay bed, Snowdrop's food bowls...

There was a twinkling fizz of golden light, and Snowdrop disappeared from her arms. Molly looked at the suddenly empty space, and giggled. She'd just done another spell! But now she had to get downstairs to see Albert! She flung open her bedroom door, and raced to the stairs.

"She looks wonderful!" Albert said admiringly, stroking Snowdrop's tummy as she lay on her back in his arms.

Molly looked round to check that Mum and Dad weren't listening. "And we cured the hiccups!" she whispered. "Snowdrop will tell you – she got a bit of a fright, and now she can't hiccup-jump any more!"

"Oh, Snowdrop, were you doing something you shouldn't? I told you to be good for Molly," Albert sighed.

"I was only a little naughty," Snowdrop yawned. "Molly is very nice, but I did miss you. You know how to peel carrots exactly right." She rubbed her ears against his sleeve lovingly.

Molly grinned at Albert. She had loved having Snowdrop as a borrowed pet, but she *was* bossy!

"Molly did well, don't you think, Albert?" Molly's dad asked, as he came out of the shed, lugging Snowdrop's hutch.

"Oh, very well. Better than you can imagine!" Albert said, smiling.

"Like I said before, Molly, I'm really proud of you." Dad glanced at Mum, and she nodded. "You know, we think you're almost ready for a pet of your own."

Molly beamed at them both, and then caught Snowdrop's eye. The silver-white rabbit's fur twinkled pink for just a second, and she winked.

Molly winked back. She was so

happy – she'd wished for a pet when Star
and Stella gave her a wish, and now it
was starting to come true. And she'd done
magic, all by herself! That was almost
as exciting. Perhaps she'd be able to use
her spells to help another magical animal
soon...

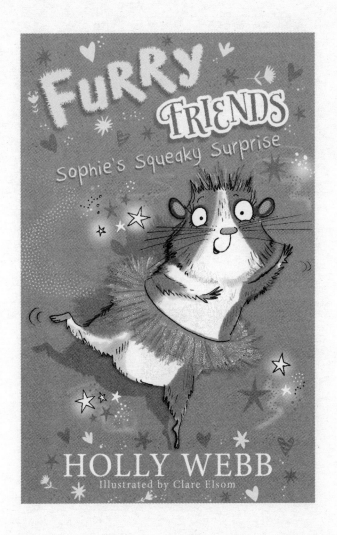

Turn over for an extract from Holly Webb's brand new series about Sophie and her super squeaky and furry friends!

CHAPTER ONE

Sophie peered out over the view, watching the sunlight sparkle on the windows, and wondering who lived there, under the roofs. She couldn't see her own house from here, or she didn't think she could, anyway. She hadn't lived in Paris for long enough to know.

The city *was* very beautiful, but it still
didn't feel like home. Sophie sighed, and
rested her chin on her hands. She missed
her old house, and her old bedroom, and
her cat, Oscar. Grandma was looking

after him while they lived in Paris, but Sophie was sure that Oscar missed her, almost as much as she missed him.

"What are you looking at?" Dan squashed up next to her, leaning over the stone balcony.

"Just things," Sophie said vaguely. "The view."

"Boring," Dan muttered. "This is taking ages. And I'm hungry." He turned round, holding his tummy in both hands and made a starving face at Sophie. His nose scrunched up like a rabbit's, and Sophie smirked. She crossed her eyes and poked her tongue out at the corner of her mouth to make Dan laugh. After all, even a wonderful view can be boring when you've been looking at it for a *VERY LONG TIME*.

All the people who live in Paris love their city so much, and many of them walk up the steep steps to the church on their wedding days to have their photographs taken next to the wonderful view. But it can take an awful long time to get the photographs right, especially when it's windy and your auntie's wedding dress won't stay still properly.

"Sophie and Dan! Stop making faces like that! You're making Dad giggle, and he's supposed to be taking romantic photos!" Mum glared at them, but Dad rolled his eyes, and stuck his tongue out at Dan. Sophie thought Dad might be a bit bored with the photos as well.

This church was one of Sophie's favourite places in Paris. It was so pretty, and there was the fountain to look at, and all the people. She even liked its name, *Sacré Coeur*, which meant Sacred Heart. Sophie thought it was very special to have a whole church that was all about love. Auntie Lou's wedding had been beautiful too, but Sophie had got up early for Mum to curl her hair and fuss over her dress, and she was tired of having to stand still and smile.

"Go and play," Auntie Lou suggested.

"Go and run around for a bit. You can come back and be in the photos later."

"Later?" Dad moaned. "I thought we'd nearly finished!" But Sophie and Dan were already halfway down the white marble steps, and couldn't hear him.

"I wish we'd brought a ball..." Dan said, as they stopped in front of the fountain that stood below the balcony. He was looking at the grassy slope of the hill. "Do you think Mum would mind if we went home and got one? It wouldn't take five minutes."

"Yes, she would! And anyway, even *you* couldn't play football on that grass," Sophie pointed out. "It would just roll down to the bottom."

"Exactly. That would make it more fun! Uphill football, I've just invented it. I might be famous!"

Sophie shook her head. "I don't think all the people taking photos would be very impressed either. There are loads of them. They'd tell you off."

"Huh." But Dan looked round at all the visitors, and realized Sophie was right. No one looked as if they wanted to play football. And there was an old lady sitting on the bench over there with a really pointy umbrella, the kind with a parrot's head handle. She looked like she'd happily use the pointy end to stab footballs, and even the parrot seemed to be giving him a fierce glare.

"Race you up and down the balustrades then!" He grabbed her hand and hurried her down the two flights of stairs to the path.

Sophie squirmed. The balustrades were the stone slopes at the sides of the steps. They were wide and flat, and Dan loved to run up and down them. He'd discovered the game the first time they came to visit the church, just after they'd moved to Paris, and since *Sacré Coeur* was on their way home from school, he'd been practising. But the game made Sophie feel sick, especially when it had been raining and the stone was all slick and slippery. She was sure that he would fall off.

"Come on, Sophie!" Dan hopped up to the stonework. "You get up on the other side. Bet I can beat you back to the top!"

Sophie stood on the bottom step, looking anxiously at the flat white slope. She didn't want to run up it – but if she refused, Dan would keep on and on teasing her.

"Baby!" her brother called scornfully, and Sophie scowled. She was only a year younger than Dan! She was not a baby! Carefully, the tip of her tongue sticking out between her teeth, she stepped on to the balustrade. It wasn't really so very high, after all… And Dan looked so surprised that she'd done it! Sophie grinned at him.

"Go!" Dan yelled, dashing away up the slope. Sophie gasped, and raced after him,

wishing she had trainers on, and not her
best shoes with the glittery bows.

She slithered a little, and gasped and
reached out her hands to balance,
wishing there was something to hold on
to – a tree maybe. But there was only
the perfect short green grass, and every

so often those funny little cone-shaped bushes that almost looked like upside-down ice creams.

Halfway to the top, Dan let out a yell as he spotted one of his friends from school on the other side of the hill. He hopped down and raced across the grass to see Benjamin, leaving Sophie glaring after him. He'd just abandoned their race, after she'd been brave enough to climb the balustrade at last. How could he? She folded her arms and tapped her foot crossly on the stone. Brothers! They were so rude!

If only she had a friend to play with, too. It wasn't fair. Sophie watched Dan and Benjamin chasing each other across the grass, and sighed sadly. Somehow, she just hadn't found anybody she liked that much at school yet. Even though Mum had spoken French to them ever since they were little, Sophie still felt as though she wasn't doing it quite right. The teachers told her she was doing ever so well, but the girls in her class looked at her funny whenever she opened her mouth. And then they just ran off. After some days at school, Sophie wondered if she might forget how to talk at all. It was nothing like back home. Mum had suggested sending emails to her friends from their school in London, and Sophie had, but it wasn't the same at all. All the fun things that Elizabeth and Zara told her in their replies only made Sophie feel more left out.

The only girls who'd really spoken to her were Chloe and Adrienne, and that was because their teacher had asked them to look after the new girl. Sophie had decided halfway through the first morning that she'd much rather be unlooked-after. Chloe didn't do anything except twitch her nose and giggle, which was boring, though bearable, but Sophie thought

Adrienne was possibly the nastiest person she had ever met. Because her voice was so sweet and soft, the things she said sounded perfectly nice at first. It was only when Sophie thought back that she realized how horrible they actually were.

"So, why *did* you move here?" Adrienne had a way of looking at Sophie with her head on one side that made Sophie feel like she was some ugly sort of beetle.

"Your French is quite good. For an English person, I mean..."

"I suppose that's an *English* skirt. It's very ... interesting."

Sophie gave a little shiver, even though the sun was warm on her bare shoulders. It was a hot September afternoon, but Adrienne's pretty voice was like cold water trickling down her spine, even when she was only remembering it.

She sighed again, and then shuddered as Dan and Benjamin started a race, rolling down the grassy slope.

And then she fell off.

Afterwards, Sophie wasn't quite sure how she did it. She hadn't even been moving. But her feet seemed to slip suddenly from underneath her, and then her arms were flapping uselessly at the air. There was a thump, and she was flat on the grass on her tummy, next to one of those strange little cone-shaped bushes.

Sophie lay there, gasping and trying not to cry. She wanted Dan to come and pick her up – but at the same time she didn't want him knowing she'd been silly enough to fall.

"Are you all right?"

It wasn't Dan. The mystery voice was speaking in French, and Dan would have spoken to her in English. It just didn't sound like Dan, anyway. Sophie hoped it wasn't the old lady with the parrot umbrella. She would probably say it was all Sophie's own fault, and insist on taking her back to Mum and Dad and

Auntie Lou and the endless photographs.

But surely even a very little old lady wouldn't have such a high, squeaky voice?

Sophie turned her head slightly, and squeaked herself.

Staring at her worriedly was a tiny furry face, ginger-and-white, with neat little ears, and shining eyes.

"Are you hurt?" the squeaky voice said again, and this time there was no doubt about it. It was definitely this small furry person who was talking to her.

"No, I'm not. Thank you for asking,"

Sophie whispered, trying to sit up.

"Oh, good. Yes, that's right. Much better." The guinea pig – for now that she was the right way up, Sophie could see that's what the furry little person was – nodded approvingly. "You didn't hit your head?"

"I don't think so," Sophie murmured, shaking it gently. Though if she had bumped her head, it would explain why she was talking to a guinea pig. And, more importantly, how the guinea pig seemed to be talking back.

"Are you imaginary?" she asked, wondering if she had actually hit her head *very hard*.

"Certainly not!" The guinea pig's voice became even squeakier. Sophie was surprised it could manage it. "Whatever gave you that idea?" it asked indignantly.

"Well. You're talking. And … and you've got a pink ballet skirt on."

The guinea pig looked down at her middle – now she'd noticed the skirt, Sophie was guessing that the guinea pig was probably a girl. Then she flounced the skirt with her little pink paws and did a twirl, gazing at her plump middle with a great deal of satisfaction. "I know. I found it yesterday. Do you like it? I think it suits me very well. But I suppose you haven't seen that many guinea pigs wearing clothes before. I can see why you'd be surprised."

"Actually, my friend Elizabeth from home is always trying to dress up her hamster," Sophie admitted. "But he bites her, every time. It was really the talking that seemed so unusual."

"Oh..." The guinea pig looked faintly worried, and her tiny round ears twitched. "It's just possible that I shouldn't have spoken to you. It *is* meant to be a secret, actually. But I was frightened that you were hurt. You were lying so still. I'm sure the others will understand." She smoothed the pink net of her skirt with anxious little pats of her paws.

"I promise I won't tell anybody," Sophie said quickly. "It was very nice of you to be worried about me." Then she frowned. "But if you're supposed to be a secret, should you be standing there like that? Everyone can see you."

The guinea pig let out a panicked

breath of a squeak. "Mercy me! I haven't even got my hat on! Do excuse me a moment." She whisked round, and disappeared under the little cone-shaped bush in a blur of ginger fur and shocking-pink net.

A minute later she was back, with a neat circle of grass attached to the top of her head. It was held on with a green ribbon, tied in a large bow under her chin.

"We'll be all right now," the guinea pig told Sophie. "Thank you for noticing, I can't think how I came to be so careless. I'll forget my own name next. It's Josephine," she added. "I didn't tell

you, did I?" She
bobbed Sophie
a little curtsey,
holding out the
ballet skirt with
her paws.

Sophie looked
around nervously. She
wasn't sure that the grassy hat was
actually enough of a disguise. The
guinea pig still looked very much like
a guinea pig, except that now she had
long green tufty hair. There were people
climbing the stone steps past them all the
time. She wondered if she should offer to
let the guinea pig hide under the edge of

her skirt. "It's very nice to meet you. I'm Sophie. But..."

"I promise..." A little pink paw was resting on Sophie's lap. "No one will see. We've been here for so many years, you know. And no one ever does notice us. After all, it's such a silly story! A family of guinea pigs living underneath the beautiful church of *Sacré Coeur*? No one would ever believe it!"